MW01069955

Presented to

Victor

from

B. B

"Happy Valentines Day."

February 14 **19** 95

Dear Parents:

This book is written for the preschool-age child. The story is fun, simple, and predictable. Young children will delight in this camping adventure with Barney, Baby Bop, and their forest friends.

We consider books to be life-long gifts that develop and enhance the love of reading. One of the best and easiest ways to help your child love books and reading is to read to your child regularly. The time together is time well spent. We hope you enjoy reading along with Barney!

Mary Ann Dudko, Ph.D.
Margie Larsen, M.Ed.
Early Childhood Educational Specialists

Art Director: Karen Malzeke-McDonald

©1993 by The Lyons Group

300 East Bethany Drive, Allen, Texas 75002

Barney™ and Baby Bop™ are trademarks of The Lyons Group.

Printed in the United States of America. All rights reserved. No part of this publication may be reproduced, stored in a retrieval system or transmitted, in any form or by any means, electronic, mechanical, photocopying, recording or otherwise, without prior written permission of the publisher.

1 2 3 4 5 6 7 8 9 10   97 96 95 94 93

ISBN 1-57064-009-2

Library of Congress Number 93-77870

A Tent Too Full

Written by Stephen White
Illustrated by Darren McKee and Bill Alger

with
Barney™ & Baby Bop™

One summer day, Barney and Baby Bop
went camping.
"I want to see lots of animals!" said Baby Bop.
"Oh, you will," said Barney. "This forest
is their home."

"And I want to sleep in a real tent!" said Baby Bop. Barney said, "I know! That's why we brought a tent that is *just* the right size for two dinosaurs."

Later, Barney and Baby Bop had fun taking a nature walk. A warm breeze blew through the leaves on the trees and made the wildflowers dance.

That night they made a campfire and ate roasty toasty marshmallows. Baby Bop still hadn't seen any forest animals.
"Maybe tomorrow," Barney said.

Soon, the sound of crickets told Barney and Baby Bop it was bedtime. They brushed their teeth and put on their pajamas.

As Barney put out the campfire, Baby Bop felt
a drop of rain, and another, and *another!*
"Don't worry about the rain," said Barney.
"We'll be warm and dry in our tent."

Barney and Baby Bop listened to the rain
make *pit-pat, split-splat* sounds on the tent.
But then they heard a new sound.
A tiny voice said, "May I **please** come in?"

It was a little wet firefly. "If you let me share your
dry tent, I can share my light with you!" he said.
"Of course we'll share our tent," Barney said.
"Come on in!"

Before long, a mother opossum and her babies were at the door. "If you let us share your dry tent," she said, "I can share the lullabies I sing for my babies."
"Oh, yes," said Baby Bop.
"Come on in!"

Next, a brown beaver came to visit. "With my strong teeth, I can chew wood!" he said. "If you let me share your dry tent, I can share some wood for your campfire." Barney said, **"Come on in!"**

"Hello," said a large moose. "If you let me share your dry tent, I can share my antlers—they're great for hanging things on!"
Barney said, **"Come on in!"**

Next, a fox came.
"If you let me share your dry tent, I can share the secret
of where to find the tastiest berries in the forest!"
Everyone was glad to say, "**Come on in!**"

Suddenly, an owl fluttered in. "Hoo-Hoo!" called the owl.
"If you let me share your dry tent, I can share my strong
voice. If anyone comes to your door, I can ask,
'Who, Who, Who is there?' "
Baby Bop said, **"Come on in!"**

"Gee," said Barney, "I think there IS someone else at the door!"
"Who, Who, Who is there?" asked the owl.
"Just me," said a brown bear. "If you let me share your dry tent, I can share my warm fur to keep everyone snuggly."

"We'll be happy to share," said Barney. Everyone bunched and scrunched to make more room. The bear squeezed and squirmed and twisted and turned.

Finally, *everyone* was inside the warm, dry tent.

"I don't think there's room for even one more friend," said a sleepy Baby Bop. Then there was a small voice at the door.
"May I *please* come in?"

It was a young raccoon with a black mask around her eyes. Barney asked, "Are you all wet too?"
"No," replied the raccoon, "I'm not wet. The rain has stopped. But I'm lonely. All the forest animals are gone!"

"No, they aren't," laughed Barney. "They are just waiting for the rain to stop!" Out tumbled the bear, owl, fox, moose, beaver, mother opossum and her babies...and finally, the tiny firefly!"

And that night, all of the forest friends slept outside under the starry sky.

And Barney and Baby Bop slept in a real tent that was *just* the right size for two dinosaurs.